Where Is Hollywood?

by Dina Anastasio

illustrated by Tim Foley

Penguin Workshop
An Imprint of Penguin Random House

For Jason—DA

For Jim—TF

PENGUIN WORKSHOP
Penguin Young Readers Group
An Imprint of Penguin Random House LLC

Library of Congress Cataloging-in-Publication Data is available.

ISBN 9781524786441 (paperback)   10 9 8 7 6 5 4 3 2 1
ISBN 9781524786458 (library binding) 10 9 8 7 6 5 4 3 2 1

Contents

Elizabeth Taylor

Where Is Hollywood?

On April 2, 1974, Hollywood's biggest movie stars gathered in the Los Angeles Music Center. They had come for the forty-sixth annual Academy Awards ceremony. Winners in more than twenty-one categories would receive a gold-plated, thirteen-and-a-half-inch statuette called Oscar.

The awards for best director, best actor, and best actress were announced. There was one award left. What movie would win for best picture?

David Niven, a longtime leading man in many films, appeared onstage. He was there to introduce the legendary actress Elizabeth Taylor. She was going to announce the winner for best picture, the last and most important award of the night.

But before Elizabeth Taylor came out, the audience started to laugh. Niven looked confused. He hadn't said anything funny. The audience kept laughing and clapping, so Niven glanced over his shoulder.

A man was running across the stage behind him. Two of his fingers were raised in a peace sign and . . . he was naked!

The runner dashed offstage. The audience kept laughing. Now Niven was, too. "That was almost bound to happen," he said. Everyone

knew what he meant. Running naked in public places was a silly fad in the early seventies. It was called streaking.

There have been a lot of crazy, weird moments in the history of Hollywood and the movies. But few have topped the incident with the "Streaker Guy" seen on TV by forty-five million people all over the world.

Who Is Oscar?

Before the very first Academy Awards ceremony in 1929, a team of Academy of Motion Picture Arts and Sciences designers created the model for the statuette. The story goes that a woman named Margaret Herrick, who was the Academy's librarian, saw it and stopped short, saying it looked just like her uncle Oscar.

The name stuck.

In 1939, Oscar became the official name of the little golden statue.

CHAPTER 1
Hollywoodland

In 1849, America was growing. There were thirty states. All were in the eastern half of the country. There were none in the West yet, and it didn't look like there would be any for a while.

Route of the California Trail and the famous stops along the way

California was the name of a vast stretch of land along the Pacific Ocean. Native American tribes, like the Mohave and Washoe, had lived there for thousands of years, but few white settlers had made it that far west.

Cars hadn't been invented. There were no trains in that part of the country. If you wanted to start a new life in this remote area, you had to travel by ship or covered wagon. Both ways were dangerous and took months.

California wasn't a state then. Not yet. In order for it to become one, sixty thousand settlers had to live there. At that time, there were less than eight thousand.

But after gold was discovered in Northern California, hordes of people began the rough journey westward. These prospectors dreaming of riches were called forty-niners. (The name came from the year gold was discovered—1849.) Suddenly, there were almost a hundred thousand settlers. Way more than enough to qualify for statehood.

On September 9, 1850, California became the thirty-first state in the United States of America.

United States in 1850

Most of the newcomers settled in the northern part of the new state, where the gold was. Not many came to Southern California. Those who did sent back letters about the beautiful land by the sea. The weather was warm and the sun shone bright day after day. It was perfect for farming.

By the late 1870s, traveling far distances became easier. The Transcontinental Railroad was complete. Trains were running all the way across America.

Harvey Henderson Wilcox and his wife, Daeida, known as Ida, were living in Topeka, Kansas. They were tired of harsh, snowy winters. Maybe it was time to throw away their winter

coats, sell their snow shovels, and move to a warmer place.

The Wilcoxes took one of the first trains to Los Angeles. They toured the area. Harvey had a knack for seeing what the future might hold. He was sure this city would keep growing. In time, people would start searching for more space outside of town.

Harvey and Ida visited a tiny community of farmers and ranchers a few miles to the west of Los Angeles. Acres and acres of lush green land were available to buy. Cows grazed. Crops flourished. What a perfect place to live! They returned to Topeka, packed up their belongings, headed west, and started buying land.

Before long, Harvey was selling land parcels, one piece at a time, for $150 an acre. Well-off people from the Midwest wanted to build second homes so they could spend their winters away from the cold. So Harvey bought more land, divided it up again, and sold it off. He was starting a community. Now it needed a name.

Ida Wilcox had once heard about a beautiful home in Florida. It was called Hollywood. Ida loved the name. She thought that's what they should call their new community. Soon, everyone was referring to the rural area as Hollywood.

Word began to spread. The weather was wonderful all year round. Los Angeles kept growing. In the 1880s, it was a frontier town with no paved roads. By 1900, it was a sprawling city. More than one hundred thousand people lived there. As for Hollywood, it had grown, too. In 1910, it became part of Los Angeles.

Hollywoodland

In 1923, a huge HOLLYWOODLAND sign was built in the Santa Monica Mountains. The sign was a real estate ad, meant to draw more people to the area. Originally, it had four thousand lightbulbs.

In 1949, the last four letters were taken away by the Hollywood Chamber of Commerce. The sign is still there today. Every night, the forty-five-foot-high letters shine down on Hollywood.

CHAPTER 2
Making Movies

Lots of people wanted to move to Los Angeles in the early 1900s. Among them were filmmakers in the East.

Movies were a new thing and just starting to become popular. *The Great Train Robbery* of 1903 was a landmark. It had a real story with thrilling action—a robbery, a chase scene.

It was long, too—at least for the time. *The Great Train Robbery* lasted twelve minutes. Directors in New York and New Jersey were now looking for a better place to film even longer, more involved movies. They were tired of cramped indoor studios. They needed space. They wanted to be able to do a lot of filming outdoors. Los Angeles might be perfect. The weather was great, and there were so many different kinds of scenery: mountains, canyons, deserts, the Pacific Ocean. Also, Los Angeles was far from Menlo Park, New Jersey, headquarters of Thomas Alva Edison.

Thomas Edison was one of the world's most famous inventors. In 1877, he had invented the phonograph, and in 1879, he created the electric lightbulb.

By the late 1880s, he was concentrating on inventing a camera that took moving pictures and a projector to display them on a large screen.

Moviemakers wanted to use Edison's new camera. Theater owners wanted to use his new movie projector so that many people could watch a movie at the same time.

Edison, however, was determined to keep control of his new inventions. Anyone who used his cameras or projectors had to pay him a fee. If they didn't, Edison would sue.

Some early movie directors found ways to avoid paying him. One way was to head to Los Angeles, where Edison's lawyers would have a hard time finding them.

Cecil B. DeMille had been writing plays and working on short documentaries in New York City. In 1913, he moved to Hollywood. He was planning a longer movie. A Western. But filming in New York would have been impossible. He needed many outdoor locations—mountains, countryside, vast open fields. The area around Los Angeles had all that. Plus, in the winter Los Angeles had good weather, so he wouldn't have to stop production because of rain or snow.

Cecil B. DeMille

DeMille's movie was called *The Squaw Man*. It told the story of an Englishman who travels out west and marries a Native American woman. Few directors had made movies about marriages between people of different races before. (*Squaw* was a term used back then for a Native American woman, but for a long time has been considered very disrespectful and racist.)

DeMille and his codirector, Oscar Apfel, had headquarters in a barn in Hollywood. They had

no idea that the location, at the corner of Vine Street and Selma Avenue, would later become the center of the movie capital of the world.

On December 29, 1913, they started filming. DeMille was very good at creating interesting characters, settings, and plots. Apfel knew how to film faraway shots, medium shots, and eye-level shots. All movies at that time were in black and white and were silent. No actors spoke lines. No one had figured out how to sync, or match up, the sound of words with actors' moving lips. Audiences in theaters had to read important parts of the story on cards that appeared on the screen.

Movies may have been silent, but that didn't mean there was no sound in theaters. Filmmakers often wrote musical scores. Sometimes piano players or small orchestras played the music as the movie was shown.

The Squaw Man was seventy-four minutes long. It was considered Hollywood's first feature (full-length) film. Audiences loved it.

D. W. Griffith was another director of short films who moved to Hollywood from New York. By 1914, he was directing hour-long movies. In California, he began work on a sweeping, three-hour epic called *The Birth of a Nation.*

It was about two families—one Northern, one Southern—during and after the Civil War. It followed the same characters over the course of many years. No director had done that before.

One battle scene called for hundreds of extras. Nothing like that had been filmed before.

It took three months to make *The Birth of a Nation*. Griffith used new camera techniques:

D. W. Griffith

close-ups, fade-outs. The actors rehearsed their scenes before filming. That was also new.

The Birth of a Nation opened on the night of February 8, 1915. It made more money than

any movie of the silent era—$18 million. That would be the same as $1.8 billion today. Its star, Lillian Gish, would become one of Hollywood's biggest silent-screen stars.

Lillian Gish

But like *The Squaw Man*, *The Birth of a Nation* is no longer shown. That is because of the offensive way it portrays African Americans. (Not many black actors even appeared in it— most were white actors in blackface makeup.) The film portrays characters who are in the Ku Klux Klan, a white hate group, as good people. It is one of the most racist movies ever made. Civil rights groups protested outside of theaters showing it. Despite their biased stories, both *The Squaw Man* and *The Birth of a Nation* were very

popular. Cecil B. DeMille went on to have a long and successful career, making epic spectacles like *The Ten Commandments*. He and D. W. Griffith put Hollywood on the map. Actors and directors watched these movies, saw a future career in films for themselves, and headed to California. So did businessmen with plans to build movie studios where many films could be produced at once. There was money to be made in this exciting new business. Lots of it.

Movie Palaces

The first movie theaters were small, dreary, and had uncomfortable seats. But that began to change in February 1913, when the Regent Theatre opened in New York City. It was as luxurious as a Broadway theater where live plays were staged. There were blue velvet carpets, satin panels on the walls, and seats for more than 1,800 people. Soon, other movie

Regent Theatre

palaces were built all over America—four thousand between 1914 and 1922. By 1939, there were fifteen thousand movie theaters. They were advertised as making "the average person feel like royalty." Many still exist and show movies today, including two of the most famous—Grauman's Chinese Theatre in Los Angeles and Radio City Music Hall in New York City.

Grauman's Chinese Theatre

CHAPTER 3
The Big Five

Louis B. Mayer owned many movie theaters in New England. He also owned a company that rented films to movie theaters. That company decided which films were shown at which theaters. Mayer bought the rights to rent out *The Birth of a Nation*. He hadn't seen it, but he knew it would be a moneymaker. That got him thinking. Maybe there were other ways he could make money in this business.

Louis B. Mayer

In 1916, he helped form a New York talent agency called Metro Pictures Corporation. Then he signed up writers, directors, and actors to work on new films, films that he would produce. And he didn't stop there.

By 1924, Mayer's company, renamed MGM (Metro-Goldwyn-Mayer, with a roaring lion for its logo), had moved to Southern California. It was a complete studio. Everything and everyone needed to make a movie worked right there. Besides directors, screenwriters, and actors, the studio hired makeup artists, costume designers, lighting technicians, camera operators, and set builders. Everybody was under contract.

On the back lot by the studio offices were big sets for filming outdoor scenes. MGM began churning out award-winning movies with the stars Mayer had signed up.

Adolph Zukor was another New Yorker who realized movies were about to change America.

Adolph Zukor

In 1916, he went out to California and started Paramount Pictures in Hollywood. Besides live-action movies, Paramount also produced popular cartoons with characters such as Betty Boop and Popeye.

Zukor wanted to be in charge of everything at his studio. He also believed in creating "star power." His talent agents would search for young actresses and actors who could be turned into famous movie stars. Zukor had them sign seven-year contracts. During that time, they couldn't work for other movie studios unless Zukor agreed to "loan them out." Many young actors and actresses were happy with this arrangement. It got their careers started. But some changed their minds later, when Paramount wouldn't let them appear in movies by other studios that offered better parts and more money.

Some of the studios owned chains of theaters. That meant there was never a problem about where and when they could show their movies.

Adolph Zukor figured out a way to have control over movie theaters that his studio didn't own. Naturally, theaters wanted to book movies with Paramount stars like Gloria Swanson, Rudolph Valentino, Greta Garbo, Mary Pickford, and Charlie Chaplin. These were the big names audiences came to see.

Movies with "star power" were called *A movies*. Zukor wouldn't let theaters rent A movies unless they also rented a Paramount cartoon, newsreel, short film, and low-budget B movie, which had no famous stars. Zukor's plan became known as block booking. It was all or nothing.

By the end of the twenties, there were five important studios in Hollywood, "the Big Five."

Besides MGM and Paramount, there was Warner Bros., started by four brothers in 1918, two of whom produced the movies and two who handled the business end. A brilliant film producer named Darryl F. Zanuck, along with Joseph M. Schenck and William Fox, headed Twentieth Century Fox, and David Sarnoff was the top guy at RKO. These big studios were each churning out about sixty to seventy movies a year. They basically controlled the film business.

The first big studio heads were all white men. Hollywood became known as a white men's club. With a few exceptions, it has stayed that way.

CHAPTER 4
The Silent Era

The movie business was booming in the 1920s. *The Big Parade* opened in 1925. By 1930 it had brought in more than $5 million, even though tickets only cost about twenty cents. Charlie Chaplin's 1925 movie, *The Gold Rush,* brought in more than $4 million in a few years. Successful directors and actors were building fancy mansions and driving expensive cars.

Fans didn't just go to the movies. They also bought movie magazines. They were eager to read about silent-film stars like Mary Pickford, Rudolph Valentino, and Clara Bow.

Dark and handsome, Rudolph Valentino starred in romantic movies like *The Sheik*. There were reports that women in theaters fainted at the sight of him on-screen. Sadly, he died after an operation

Rudolph Valentino

when he was only thirty-one. Thousands of people came to his funeral in New York City.

Clara Bow was called the "It Girl" after starring in a hit movie called *It*. Some people thought she was vulgar because of the way she dressed and danced and partied. She was too wild, they said. But this was the Jazz Age—the Roaring Twenties. Many young women wanted to look exactly like Clara Bow.

Clara Bow

The Hays Code

Some Americans objected to sexy scenes and bad language in movies. So in 1930, a set of moral guidelines was put in place. It was called the Hays Code after Will Hays, president of the Motion Picture Producers and Distributors of America. Movies couldn't be too scary. Too sexy. Have too much drinking or violence. Use bad words.

Many producers ignored the strict code at first. But by 1934, they were following it. The Hays Code continued through Hollywood's golden age and the early years of television. It influenced later movies and officially ended in 1968.

THIS PICTURE APPROVED BY THE PRODUCTION CODE ADMINISTRATION OF THE MOTION PICTURE PRODUCERS & DISTRIBUTORS OF AMERICA.

CERTIFICATE NO.

Mary Pickford, by contrast, was known as "America's Sweetheart." She was married to the dashing actor Douglas Fairbanks, who starred in action films such as *Robin Hood* and *The Mark of Zorro*. He was just as famous as his wife. They were Hollywood's royal couple.

At first, actors and actresses got no credits. But moviegoers came to know them from seeing them on-screen. So the stars demanded credit and higher salaries. Soon, the most popular stars became rich. Like many successful stars, Fairbanks and Pickford lived in Beverly Hills, not far from where they made their movies. In 1919, they bought a remote eighteen-acre property. They turned it into a lavish home called Pickfair.

Although hardly anyone—even the rich—had a pool at that time, the one at Pickfair was so big, people could canoe in it! Pickfair became the second most famous home in America, after the White House. The couple was famous for

their extravagant lawn parties. Everyone wanted to be invited. Silent-film stars were photographed driving through the gate, playing tennis, riding the Pickfair horses, zooming down the pool slide.

Charlie Chaplin was friends with Pickford and Fairbanks. He was not only a famous actor, he also wrote and directed his movies—*Easy Street, The Kid, The Gold Rush, The Circus*. He created a character called the Little Tramp. The good-natured hobo who behaved like a gentleman

became one of America's most beloved silent-film characters.

Charlie Chaplin liked Pickfair so much, he built his own sprawling home across the road.

Silent movies had made Fairbanks, Pickford, and Chaplin rich. Now they were ready to make sure they were in charge of their careers. They wanted to choose what movies they made and how they

The Little Tramp

made them. So in 1919, they started their own studio, United Artists, with D. W. Griffith.

Life for Hollywood stars was good. It couldn't get better. But then, on October 6, 1927, a movie from Warner Bros. called *The Jazz Singer* opened. It was about a boy who wants to be a jazz singer, but his father wants him to be a cantor singing prayers at the synagogue. The movie starred Al Jolson.

It was the first talking movie.

Al Jolson

The Talkies

The Jazz Singer changed the movie business. Audiences wanted more talking movies. For the  first time, moviegoers would hear the voices of their favorite stars. Al Jolson had a great singing and speaking voice. Many other actors, like John Barrymore in England and Eddie Cantor in New York, had been trained to perform before live theater audiences. They had excellent voices, too, and easily found starring roles in the talkies.

But there was a problem. Some silent stars had voices that audiences found annoying. And a few

John Barrymore

actors who had starred in Westerns had foreign accents. That wasn't going to work anymore, and some careers ended.

CHAPTER 5
Hollywood's Golden Age

In the 1930s, America was suffering through the Great Depression, the worst economic crisis in its history. For millions of people, it was hard to find work, pay the rent, or buy food.

Yet, at times, what people wanted most was to forget their worries. So when they had some extra change, they went to the movies. Most people went to a movie once a week.

The 1930s marked the beginning of what is often called the golden age of Hollywood. The movies were creative and varied. There were Westerns, slapstick comedies, musicals, and biopics (biographical movies). Many of the films now considered classics were made in this decade: *The Wizard of Oz, King Kong, Mr. Smith Goes to Washington.* In 1940, *Gone with the Wind,* about the Civil War, was awarded eight Oscars, including best picture. Hattie McDaniel won best supporting actress for her role in the movie. It was the first time an African American actor had ever taken home an Oscar.

Hattie McDaniel

Gone with the Wind

This blockbuster movie was not as openly racist as D. W. Griffiths's *The Birth of a Nation*. But it did not create a realistic depiction of the Civil War South. It portrayed rich, slave-owning Southerners as kindly, loving people who treated those in bondage almost as part of the family.

Hattie McDaniel's Oscar was for portraying Mammy, a slave who has cared for the heroine Scarlett O'Hara since childhood. McDaniel's performance was wonderful, but very few other roles were open to her. That held true for all black actors and actresses. During a long career, Hattie McDaniel played a maid seventy-four times.

During the thirties, big movie studio heads continued to hold enormous power. Most actors and actresses under contract never got beyond playing small roles in movies. But a few became rich and famous superstars, including Humphrey Bogart, Bette Davis, James Stewart, Katharine Hepburn, Spencer Tracy, and Joan Crawford.

Shirley Temple

Aspiring actors and actresses poured into Hollywood during the golden age. Parents knocked on studio doors, determined to make their child the next star. A few succeeded. Most didn't.

Shirley Temple was the first child superstar. She had blond curls and big dimples. She was totally adorable. And she could sing and dance. In 1933, she signed with Fox Film Corporation. She was five years old.

Bright Eyes, the first feature film created for a child, was released in 1934. The song Shirley sang in the film, "On the Good Ship Lollipop," became a huge hit.

Shirley Temple in *Bright Eyes*

Mickey Rooney started acting in films when he was six. Later, he made a series of very popular movies for MGM about a teenager named Andy Hardy. One of his costars was Judy Garland. Judy's real name was Frances Ethel Gumm. Like many other stars, her name was changed when she signed with the big studio.

Many child stars had a very hard time. Louis B. Mayer made his child stars work long, eighteen-hour days and nights. When they weren't working, they took lots of lessons: dancing, singing, horseback-riding, swimming. Anything they might need to do in a movie. Judy Garland became one of Hollywood's biggest young stars

after playing Dorothy in *The Wizard of Oz*. At seventeen, she was already a natural and convincing actress who had a rich, emotional singing voice.

Judy Garland as Dorothy in *The Wizard of Oz*

But Mayer wanted her to lose weight. So she was given dangerous pills as a way to diet. Sadly, she became addicted to them. After a rocky life and career, she died in 1969, at age forty-seven.

It wasn't until 1948 that the studios lost some control over the movie industry. The US government decided that Hollywood studios had too much power. Some owned chains of movie theaters. Independent theaters often couldn't rent the best movies from studios, or they didn't get them until months after they came out. That wasn't fair. Nor was the studios' system of block booking their movies. Small, independent filmmakers had the odds stacked against them. Their movies couldn't get into any of the theaters owned by studios.

The government took the big studios to court. The government won. The studios were forced to sell their theaters. Now the new theater owners could pick whatever movies they wanted. Theaters began showing more films made by independent producers.

After decades of almost total power, the Big Five lost their iron grip.

Back Lots

Movie companies built back lots next to their offices and indoor soundstages. On a back lot, sets were created—for example, a street in a town of the Old West, a haunted house, a beach, a nightclub. *Tarzan the Ape Man* was filmed on a jungle lot. Andy Hardy movies used a small town square lot. *Frankenstein* and *Dracula* from Universal Studios were filmed on a lot that looked like a little European village.

Some back lot sets were ripped down after one movie was made. Others were reused many times. One of the most famous was the RKO Forty Acres lot. In 1933, *King Kong* was made there. A few years later, producer David O. Selznick rented the Forty Acres lot for his movie *Gone with the Wind.* He created brand-new sets for Tara and the Twelve Oaks plantations, for a railroad station, and for the city of Atlanta (which gets burned down).

CHAPTER 6
Disney

One of the most successful movie studios ever had superstars that never got paid. Not a penny. That's because they were cartoon characters.

Walt Disney had always loved cartoons. When he was a kid, he practiced copying the pictures in newspaper cartoon strips. When he was older,

Walt was the cartoonist for his high-school newspaper.

In 1919, Walt and his friend Ub Iwerks got jobs at a company that made short animated films. Animation—cartoons in action—was new.

Walt was hooked. He would create movies with great characters that moved.

Animation took a lot of time. To make an animated film, cartoonists had to draw hundreds of images for every scene. How did they show a character waving? One picture was drawn with a hand slightly raised. In the next, the hand was moved a tiny bit to one side. The next drawing showed it even a little farther to the side. And so on. It takes 1,400 different pictures to create a minute's worth of animated action.

In 1923, Walt moved to Hollywood and started Disney Brothers Studio with his brother Roy. It wasn't long before he was making money from short animated films. In 1928, he released

the black-and-white short film *Steamboat Willie*.
It starred a mouse called Mickey. More Mickey
Mouse shorts followed.

Mickey Mouse was
Walt Disney's first
Hollywood superstar.
Donald Duck was
next. Disney had a
monopoly on kids'
movies.

In 1932, Disney
made the first full-
color animated short
film. It was called *Flowers and Trees*. Then, in
1938, Walt released *Snow White and the Seven
Dwarfs*, which was longer. It was the first full-
length animated feature film, and also the first
one in color. *Snow White* was followed by other
animated Technicolor hits—*Bambi*, *Dumbo*, and
Pinocchio.

In the 1950s, Walt started making live-action films—ones with real actors, not animated characters. Once again, he found box office gold with a string of hits: *Old Yeller*, *Treasure Island*, *Davy Crockett*, *Kidnapped*, *Pollyanna*, and *Swiss Family Robinson*.

Today, the Walt Disney Company is a huge Hollywood business. It owns Marvel, Lucasfilm (which makes the *Star Wars* films), and the Pixar studio, which has turned out animated superhits like *Toy Story*, *Finding Nemo*, and *Wall-E*. And in 2013, Disney released a new "princess" animated movie like the classics it had created in the past. It was called *Frozen*, with *Frozen 2* following in 2019.

Elsa from *Frozen*

Movies in Color

Color was added to black-and-white motion pictures as far back as 1902. However, not until 1932, with the introduction of Technicolor, did producing realistic full-color motion pictures become possible. At first, Technicolor film was used primarily for home movies. *Becky Sharp* (1935) was the first commercial movie shot in three-strip Technicolor. Four years later, two blockbuster films came out that were noted for their amazing Technicolor images—*Gone with the Wind* and *The Wizard of Oz.*

CHAPTER 7
Hollywood Goes to War

In December 1941, the United States joined World War II. By this time, Adolf Hitler and his Nazi party had invaded many countries in Europe. Japan became allies with Germany. The United States was determined to stop what became known as the Axis powers.

More than sixteen million men from all over the United States signed up to join the armed forces. They were sent to fight in countries in both Europe and the Pacific.

President Franklin D. Roosevelt saw that Hollywood could help the war effort. Young American soldiers in distant places would be taking breaks from the fighting. Sometimes they would be watching movies. Roosevelt talked to some of Hollywood's top directors. He asked them to make entertaining feature films that would keep up soldiers' spirits. As for people at home, they wanted to understand what war was really like.

The directors were happy to help. Many joined the army, navy, or marines. Some filmed battles for news agencies. Their newsreels were shown in theaters before the main movie began. Others concentrated on longer documentaries. They joined the troops in Europe and the Pacific on planes, ships, and the front lines. Director Frank Capra made the well-known *Why We Fight* series. John Huston made *Report from the Aleutians* in 1943. John Ford came out with *The Battle of*

Midway in 1942. George Stevens filmed one of World War II's most important battles—D-Day—from the warship HMS *Belfast* as it happened. These directors made movies that showed what it was really like to go to war—sometimes lonely, sometimes boring, often terrifying. After the war, they all went on to make many of Hollywood's greatest films.

Some of the best feature films of all time were made during World War II. *Casablanca*, a film about people desperate to escape from Hitler's Nazi officials in war-torn Morocco, was released in 1942. It won the Academy Award for best picture.

Directors weren't the only people in Hollywood helping the war effort. Many actors sold war bonds that helped pay for things the military needed. Major stars like James Stewart and Henry Fonda enlisted and headed off to fight. Some actresses joined the Red Cross. They cared for the sick and the wounded. Al Jolson and Bob Hope flew overseas to entertain American troops.

In California, cities were crowded with

servicemen waiting to be shipped to islands in the Pacific. They needed a place to stay. Hollywood welcomed them. "Mom" Lehr's Hollywood Guild and Canteen provided meals and beds for thousands. Every night, up to 1,200 servicemen gathered at the Hollywood Canteen. Big bands played swing music, and many Hollywood stars entertained.

The Hollywood Canteen

When the war finally ended in 1945, the film industry was different. War had changed many returning actors and directors. They wanted to make more serious movies.

After World War II, the Soviet Union and the United States were the two world superpowers—and they were bitter enemies. The Soviet Union was a Communist dictatorship. In a Communist state, no one owns property or businesses. The state owns everything and is supposed to see to people's needs. There are no free elections.

The United States was scared that the Soviet Union was not only trying to take over other countries but was also placing a network of spies inside the United States. One senator, Joseph McCarthy from Wisconsin, suspected that Hollywood producers were slipping Communist messages into movies. He held hearings, and many Hollywood directors, film stars, and screenwriters had to appear before Congress. They were asked to say if they— or anyone they knew—were Communists. The US Constitution says anyone can believe whatever they want. But the McCarthy hearings were trying to get rid of that right.

Joseph McCarthy

The Blacklist

In 1950, ten filmmakers were sentenced to up to a year in jail because they wouldn't say what their beliefs were, nor would they reveal the names of any people who might be Communists. It was a terrible time in Hollywood. A blacklist was circulated with names of stars, directors, editors, screenwriters, and other people in the industry suspected of being Communists. They couldn't get jobs anymore.

This time—called the Red Scare—lasted until the mid-1950s and ruined the lives of many people.

CHAPTER 8
Here Comes Television

World War II was over, but for Hollywood and the movies, there was a new danger. It was a black box with a screen that people bought and placed in their living rooms.

It was called a television.

In 1945, there was a poll. Americans were asked if they knew what television was. Most said they didn't. Very few people owned TVs. In 1950, more than six million TV sets were sold. Early shows were in black and white. There were only seven channels. Still, everyone, it seemed, wanted one. Although they were expensive to buy, once you owned a television set, all the shows were free.

Many early shows were series—comedies, mysteries, Westerns. The same characters would appear in a different episode every week. Quiz shows were popular, too.

During the 1950s, many families watched TV instead of going to the movies. Kids couldn't get enough of shows like *Hopalong Cassidy*, *Lassie*, *The Adventures of Rin Tin Tin*, and *Adventures of Superman*.

Shows for the whole family were popular, too.

Madelyn Pugh was a writer on one of TV's most-watched family shows—*I Love Lucy*. Lucille Ball and her real-life husband, Desi Arnaz, were the stars. In the show, he owned a nightclub in New York City. Lucy was always trying to find a way to perform there—or else she was cooking up some other crazy scheme to make money and get famous. Madelyn Pugh wrote many of the most famous scenes: Lucy wrestling in a vat of grapes; hanging from a balcony; gobbling chocolates faster and faster on a candy factory assembly line.

There weren't many opportunities for women writers or directors. Madelyn Pugh had started writing for radio in the early 1940s, when all the men went off to war. Many women were fired when the war was over and the men returned. But Madelyn kept writing.

By 1957, *I Love Lucy* was so successful that Lucy and Desi were able to buy RKO's old Hollywood studio and fix it up. It was renamed Desilu (for Desi and Lucy) Productions. Lucille Ball became the first woman to ever be in charge of a major television studio.

As TV changed America, many movie studios struggled. In 1946, the United States Census Bureau asked people about going out to the movies. Almost ninety million went to a movie theater once a week. By 1960, the number had dropped by more than half to only forty million.

Most studios were losing money. Were movies becoming a thing of the past?

CHAPTER 9
New Hollywood

In the early 1960s, Hollywood was still losing money.

United Artists had to sell off its back lot, which became condos and shopping malls. Universal Studios began offering tours of the studio to bring in money. With the passing of the original studio heads, their companies were bought up by big businesses—such as banks—that had never made movies.

Walt Disney Productions, however, was doing very well. One reason was that it was now in the television business, too. It produced popular kids' shows, such as *Walt Disney's Disneyland*, *Walt Disney Presents*, *Zorro*, and *The Mickey Mouse Club*.

Universal Studios tour trolley

Other studios followed suit, creating television studios. But that wasn't going to help filmmaking. Hollywood movies had to change; they had to offer something different from what they had in the past, and also something different from the entertainment shown on TV.

America was changing in the 1960s. It was a time of upheaval. There were protests against the war in Vietnam, and marches for civil rights, women's rights, and gay rights. It was a decade

that saw the assassination of many leaders—John F. Kennedy, Martin Luther King Jr., and Robert Kennedy. It was a confusing time, and Hollywood tried to deal with the changes.

In 1967, *Guess Who's Coming to Dinner* was released. It wasn't a particularly great movie. But it was about a young white woman who brings her African American boyfriend home to meet her parents. The boyfriend was played by Sidney Poitier, one of Hollywood's most gifted actors. A few

Sidney Poitier

years earlier, he had become the first black man to win the Oscar for best actor. (It was for a movie called *Lilies of the Field*.) Today, the subject of an interracial romance would not be newsworthy, but it was groundbreaking in the sixties.

Some of the most interesting films were made in Europe and shown in small movie houses in the United States. They didn't have strict rules about violence, language, or sexuality. Their movies didn't always end happily. Young Americans liked them.

In 1968, the Hays Code was replaced with a rating system. Movies would no longer be censored. Instead, they were assigned different letter ratings that alerted moviegoers as to whether the movie contained sex, violence, and adult language. Parents would know that a movie with a G (General Audience) rating was suitable for young children, while a PG movie required more guidance. In 1984, the PG-13 rating was introduced. These films might not be appropriate for children under thirteen.

Two 1967 American-made movies proved there was a big audience for sophisticated material. *The Graduate*, directed by Mike Nichols, was about a recent college graduate who has an affair with an older married woman. *Bonnie and Clyde* told the story of two young gangsters in the 1930s who go on a violent bank-robbing spree. The final scene, showing their bloody deaths in a shoot-out, was

Faye Dunaway and Warren Beatty in *Bonnie and Clyde*

filmed as if it were a ballet in slow motion. As for the studios, now, instead of making a movie themselves, they might put up the money for films made by young independent directors. In the seventies, some of the most talented directors ever began their careers.

Francis Ford Coppola came out with *The Godfather* in 1972. It was about a violent New York City crime family. It showed gangsters as real people with real problems and real feelings. Paramount was financing the film. The studio heads wanted to use actors with star power. Coppola insisted on young actors, like Diane Keaton, Al Pacino, James Caan, and Robert Duvall. Paramount decided to take a chance.

The Godfather made more money than any other movie that year. It won the Academy Award for best picture. *The Godfather Part II* was released two years later. It, too, won the Academy Award for best picture.

James Caan and Al Pacino

Hollywood Walk of Fame

On March 28, 1960, a five-pointed pink terrazzo star was placed in the sidewalk on Hollywood Boulevard. The name on the star was Stanley Kramer, a famous Hollywood director. It was the first star on one of the world's most well-known walkways—the Hollywood Walk of Fame. Today, more than 2,500 stars (even fictional characters like Mickey Mouse) line Hollywood Boulevard and Vine Street. People can get a star for work in five categories: motion pictures, television, music, radio, and theater/live performance.

Some people have more than one star. Michael Jackson has his own star, and one for the Jacksons.

As a teenager growing up in Arizona, Steven Spielberg made up stories and turned them into short films using a family movie camera. Making movies was the only thing he ever wanted to do.

Spielberg was twenty-seven years old when he read Peter Benchley's exciting novel *Jaws*. The book was about a huge great white shark that

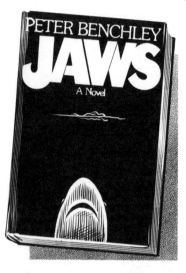

attacks people in a small beach town on a July Fourth weekend. It would make a really terrifying— and terrific—movie. It would be a different kind of horror film.

Two producers at Universal wanted to make the movie. Spielberg was interested in directing it, and he got the job. He decided to film *Jaws* on Martha's Vineyard, an island off Massachusetts in the Atlantic Ocean.

Spielberg soon learned that making movies in open water is really hard. Bad weather caused delay after delay. Rough seas made it impossible to shoot. The mechanical shark kept breaking.

At one point, Universal threatened to shut the picture down. But the studio decided to let Spielberg keep going.

Jaws finally opened in June 1975. Everyone, including Steven Spielberg, had pretty much given up on it being a hit. They were wrong. It wasn't just a hit. It was one of Hollywood's first summer blockbusters, a mega-moneymaker. The ads said: "You'll never go in the water again!" Audiences watched, thrilled and terrified, as the killer shark approached its next victim. The ads had been right. Lots of people were now petrified to go near the ocean.

Since the midseventies, Steven Spielberg has gone on to make countless modern classics such as *E.T.*, the Indiana Jones movies, *Schindler's List*, and *Lincoln*.

Like Spielberg, George Lucas was a young director who was excited about exploring new ideas. He had grown up in California, reading comic books and watching space adventures and Westerns on TV. He was obsessed with figuring out how things worked and inventing gadgets. When he was a teenager, George started taking pictures. At the University of Southern California film school, he learned about directing, acting, editing, special effects, and the importance of music.

While a student, George won a Warner Bros. scholarship to study under one of its directors. He was assigned to Francis Ford Coppola. In

1971, George started his own film studio. It was called Lucasfilm, and it was located outside of San Francisco, not in Hollywood. He was imagining a movie that would be a cross between a Western and a space fantasy.

Like the original Hollywood studio heads, George wanted to be in control of all aspects of his movie. He wrote the script and searched for a larger studio willing to put up the money while still leaving him his independence. His idea was to do a continuing series of movies based on the universe and characters in his head. (Before this, producers and directors planned on a sequel—a follow-up—only if the first movie was a huge hit.)

Some studios turned down George's idea. But Twentieth Century Fox agreed to do it.

Star Wars opened in late May of 1977. Audiences were amazed. This was science fiction like no one had ever seen before! It was that summer's blockbuster.

In 2012, George Lucas sold Lucasfilm to the Walt Disney Company. The eighth episode of *Star Wars*, called *Star Wars: The Last Jedi*, was released by Disney in 2017. There are more to come. *Star Wars* has become so much a part of our culture that it is hard to imagine a time before there were Jedi knights.

CHAPTER 10
A Slowly Changing Hollywood

It was back in the 1880s that Harvey and Ida Wilcox built their first house in the community that became Hollywood. Today, it is a crowded neighborhood within the city of Los Angeles. More people live in LA than in any other American city, except New York City.

Movies are still filmed in and around the area of Hollywood, but many directors choose other locations, sometimes because it's cheaper. Peter Jackson, who is from New Zealand, filmed his *Lord of the Rings* movies there. *Wonder Woman* was filmed in Italy, England, and France. Besides

Peter Jackson on the set of a *Lord of the Rings* film

where movies are made, how they are made has changed drastically. That's because of technology. The key word is *digital*. Many directors today use digital cameras instead of film. Editing is done on computers. Special effects are created digitally.

Big Hollywood studios still make movies. But competition is growing.

HBO started as a cable TV channel and now makes movies. So does Netflix, which only used to deliver movies made by other companies. Amazon, which sells 40 percent of all new books in the United States, is now financing and producing movies, too.

On May 16, 1929, 270 people gathered at the Hollywood Roosevelt Hotel for the first Academy Awards ceremony. Winners in twelve categories were given gold-plated statues. The ceremony lasted fifteen minutes.

Today, many more award categories have been added. The ceremony, which has been televised since 1953, usually lasts three hours—too long, many TV viewers think!

Watching the awards show year after year makes one thing clear to viewers—the movie industry is still dominated by white men. Women and all people of color hold few of the top jobs. As of 2018, in the ninety-year history of the Oscars, only five black directors had ever been nominated for the best director award. None of them had won. Only five women had ever been nominated for the best director Oscar. Kathryn Bigelow was the only winner. She took home the Oscar in 2010 for a movie called *The Hurt Locker*. It is about soldiers in a bomb-disposal unit during the Iraq War.

After nominees were announced for the 2016 awards, lots of people grew angry. Many excellent films made by women and nonwhite filmmakers and actors had not been nominated. In particular, critics praised *Straight Outta Compton*, about Dr. Dre and his former rap group, and *Creed*, the latest movie in the *Rocky* series. And all acting nominees—both in the best actress and best actor categories—were white. All director nominees were men.

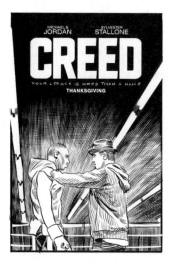

A protest movement began. It was called Oscars So White. The Academy listened. It changed the list of official voters for the awards. Almost seven hundred new members were chosen. Many were women and people of color. Most were younger.

In 2017, Oscar-nominated movies made by filmmakers of color were *Moonlight*, *Fences*, and *13th*. Seven actors and actresses of color were nominated. *Moonlight*, the story of a gay African American boy growing up in Miami, won for best picture. It was directed and coproduced by Barry Jenkins, an African American filmmaker.

Mahershala Ali won best supporting actor for the same film. And Viola Davis won best supporting actress for her role in *Fences*, about a black family in Pittsburgh, which also starred Denzel Washington.

Mahershala Ali and Viola Davis

The Oscars were "less white," but there was much more work to be done. Independent film companies like HBO, Amazon, and Netflix stepped up. Filmmakers of all races would receive funding to make more diverse movies. There would be more money for women filmmakers. How much of a difference will it make and how soon will change come? Only time will tell.

Whatever its problems, the film industry continues to do what it has been doing for more than a hundred years—creating entertainment on-screen that dazzles and entrances audiences all over the world. Sure, there are other cities that are centers for moviemaking—for example, Mumbai in India, which has become known as Bollywood.

Still, there is only one Hollywood, and it is far more than a geographic location. It is the glamour capital of the United States—the place where movie magic is made.

Timeline of Hollywood

1897 — Thomas Edison patents his movie camera, called the Kinetograph

1911 — Hollywood's first film studio, Nestor Film Company, opens

1914 — *The Squaw Man*, Hollywood's first feature-length film, is released

1915 — D. W. Griffith's *The Birth of a Nation* is released

1927 — Philo Taylor Farnsworth invents the first electronic television

— The first talkie, *The Jazz Singer*, opens

1928 — Disney's *Steamboat Willie*, introducing Mickey Mouse, is released

1929 — *Wings* wins the first Academy Award for best picture

1942 — *Casablanca* opens

1951 — *I Love Lucy* debuts on television

1960 — First Hollywood Walk of Fame star appears on Hollywood Boulevard

1964 — Sidney Poitier wins the Academy Award for best actor, the first African American man ever to win

1975 — *Jaws* opens

1977 — *Star Wars* opens

2010 — Kathryn Bigelow wins the Academy Award for best director, the first woman ever to do so

2017 — Barry Jenkins's *Moonlight* wins the Academy Award for best picture

Timeline of the World

1902 — Mary Anderson invents the windshield wiper

1903 — First Major League Baseball World Series

— Orville and Wilbur Wright fly the first successful self-propelled airplane

1914 — World War I begins

1928 — Alexander Fleming discovers penicillin

1932 — Amelia Earhart becomes the first woman to fly solo across the Atlantic Ocean

1952 — Princess Elizabeth becomes queen of England

1961 — Yuri Gagarin becomes the first person to fly into outer space

1963 — First measles vaccine administered in the United States

1967 — Christiaan Barnard performs the first human-to-human heart transplant

1969 — First message sent over the Internet

1978 — Muhammad Ali wins his third world heavyweight boxing championship

1993 — Toni Morrison wins the Nobel Prize in Literature

1994 — Nelson Mandela becomes the first black president of South Africa

2007 — First iPhone is released

2016 — Michael Phelps wins his twenty-third gold Olympic medal for swimming

— Bob Dylan wins the Nobel Prize in Literature

Bibliography

*Books for young readers

Bouzereau, Laurent, director. ***Five Came Back***. 2017. Los Angeles, CA: Amblin Television, 2017.

Capra, Frank, director. ***Why We Fight: World War II***. US War Department and Academy of Motion Picture Arts and Sciences, 1942–1945.

Friedgen, Bud, and Michael J. Sheridan, director. ***That's Entertainment! III***. 1994. Culver City, Metro-Goldwyn-Mayer, 1994.

*Frith, Margaret. ***Who Was Thomas Alva Edison?*** New York: Penguin Workshop, 2005.

Haley Jr., Jack, director. ***That's Entertainment!*** Los Angeles: Metro-Goldwyn-Mayer, 1974.

Harris, Mark. ***Five Came Back: A Story of Hollywood and the Second World War***. New York: Penguin Press, 2015.

*Holub, Joan. ***What Was the Gold Rush?*** New York: Penguin Workshop, 2013.

Kelly, Gene, director. ***That's Entertainment, Part II***. Culver City, CA: Metro-Goldwyn-Mayer, 1976.

Mariano, Paul, and Kurt Norton, directors. ***These Amazing Shadows***. San Francisco, CA: Gravitas Docufilms, 2011.

*Pollack, Pam, and Meg Belviso. ***Who Is George Lucas?*** New York: Penguin Workshop, 2014.

Scorsese, Martin, and Michael Henry Wilson, directors. *A Personal Journey With Martin Scorsese Through American Movies*. London, UK: Arte (BFI), 1995.

*Spinner, Stephanie. *Who Is Steven Spielberg?* New York: Penguin Workshop, 2013.

*Stewart, Whitney. *Who Was Walt Disney?* New York: Penguin Workshop, 2009.

Wanamaker, Marc, and Robert W. Nudelman. *Early Hollywood*. Charleston, SC: Arcadia Publishing, 2007.

Websites

American Film Institute. www.afi.com

Internet Movie Database. IMDb.com

The Official Star Wars Website. www.starwars.com

Mickey Mouse's star on the Hollywood Walk of Fame

Actors Douglas Fairbanks, Mary Pickford, and Charlie Chaplin

Warner Bros. film studios, 1930

OREGON.

IDAHO.

NEVADA

SAN FRANCISCO

CALIFORNIA

HOLLYWOOD

LOS ANGELES

PACIFIC OCEAN

WALT DISNEY STUDIOS

WARNER BROS STUDIOS

UNIVERSAL STUDIOS

UNIVERSAL STUDIOS

HOLLYWOOD

HOLLYWOOD

GRIFFITH OBSERVATORY

LOS FELIZ BLVD

HOLLYWOOD BOWL

CHINESE THEATRE

HOLLYWOOD BLVD

SUNSET BLVD

HOLLYWOOD WALK OF FAME

HOLLYWOOD PALLADIUM

SANTA MONICA BLVD.

N.HIGHLAND AVE.

VINE ST.

PARAMOUNT PICTURES STUDIO

N.WESTERN AVE.

MELROSE AVE.

SUNSET BLVD

BEVERLY HILLS

BEVERLY BLVD

WEST 3RD ST.